A
Bad Case
of
Animal
Nonsense

Published in paperback in 1995
by Orion Children's Books
a division of the Orion Publishing Group Ltd
Orion House
5 Upper St Martin's Lane
London WC2H 9EA

First published in Great Britain in 1981
by Dent Children's Books

A catalogue record for this book
is available from the British Library

Printed in Great Britain

ISBN: 1 85881 105 8

A Dolphin
Paperback

A Bad Case of Animal Nonsense

featuring The Animal Alphabet,
I Know an Old Lady,
Poems
Rhyming Animals

By Jonathan Allen

A Bad Case of Animal Nonsense was one of the first things I ever had published. And it's still one of my favourite books, so, as you can imagine, I'm dead pleased to see it being revived at long last.

It combined the three things I liked doing most, drawing mad animals, messing around with words, and making people laugh. As this is exactly what I've been doing ever since, for me *Animal Nonsense* is where it all started. I hope you derive as much pleasure from reading this book as I did from writing and illustrating it. (Although, I have to say that the lettering nearly killed me!) And as the old joke goes, if you enjoyed it half as much as I did, then I enjoyed it twice as much as you...

Best wishes

Jonathan Allen

Also by Jonathan Allen
Two by Two by Two

Contents

Rhyming Animals

Rhyming Animals

An Aardvark in a Car Park....

A Two-Toed Sloth under oath...

A Puma spreading a rumour...

Rhyming Animals

A Parakeet
with smelly
feet.

A Gnu in
a canoe.

A Flamingo playing
bingo

Oxen with socks on . . . . . .

A Wild Boar at the door. . . . .

A Hare that doesn't care. . . . .

Rhyming Animals

A Llama in a Melodrama.

A Chameleon that made a million....

A Stoat in a coat....

Bears on the stairs.

JBA 80

The Animal Alphabet

The Animal Alphabet

The hunter should never
have entered the "Alphabet Game Park",
because the animals have their
own way of dealing with hunters...

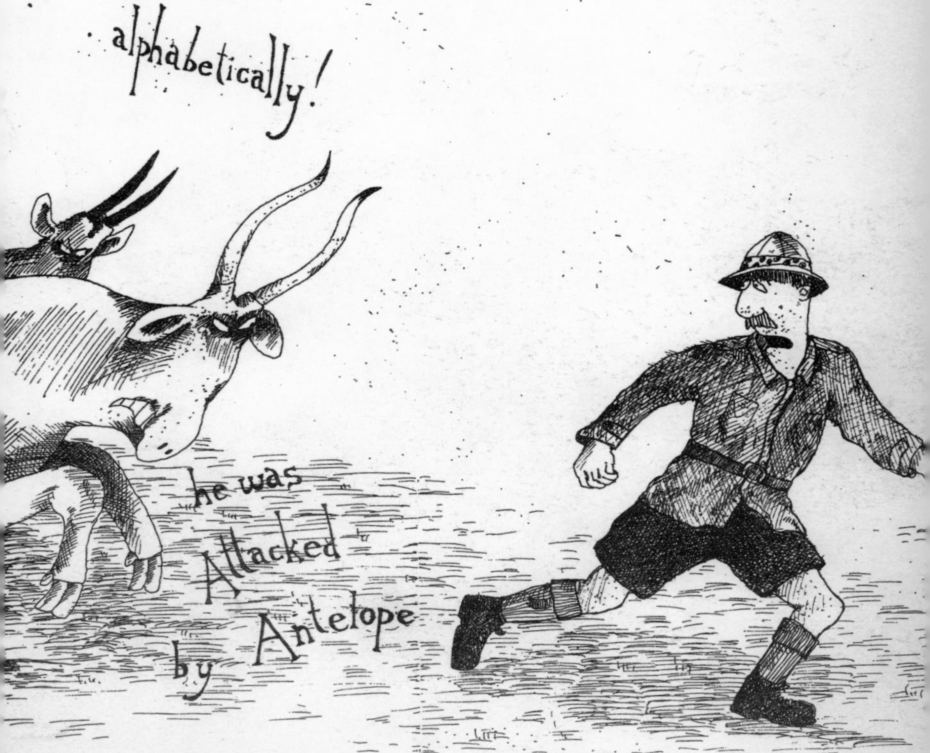
alphabetically!
he was
Attacked
by Antelope

Chided by Chipmunks

Disciplined by Dormice

Elongated by Elephants

Flattened by Foxes

Goaded by Gorillas

Hindered by Hippopotami

I

J

Jostled by Jaguars

Needled by Nilgai

Offended by Otters

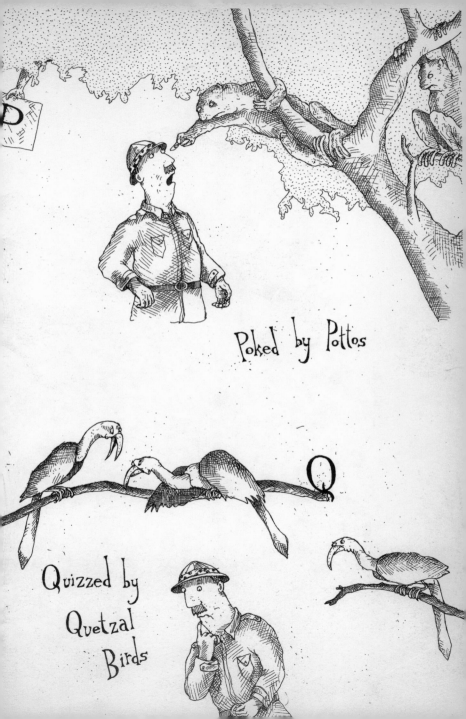

Poked by Pottos

Quizzed by
Quetzal
Birds

Rattled by Rhino

Savaged by Stoats

Trampled by Tapirs

Upset by Unicorns

Then he was
eXpelled from
the
Game Park ,

After Yielding to Yaks

I Know
an Old Lady

I Know an Old Lady

I know an old lady
Who swallowed a fly,
I don't know why
She swallowed a fly,
Perhaps she'll die...

I know an old lady
Who swallowed a bird,
How absurd,
To swallow a bird,

She swallowed the bird
To catch the spider, etc.

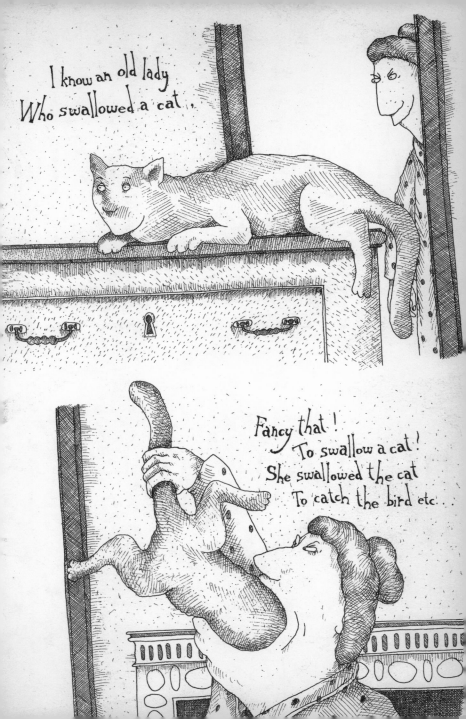

I know an old lady
Who swallowed a horse,

She's dead of course . . . . .

THE END

Animal Poems

Fortuitous Fauna

a camel in a monorail

a parrot in a lift

a rabbit on a motorbike home from its nightshift

a budgie with a sten gun holding up a bank

an aardvark in a dressing gown

a badger in a tank

a. possum on the underground...

a panda in the bath...

a herd of smiling kangaroos hopping up your path...

a gerbil playing basketball...

with gibbons, mice, and bears

stoats on bikes, and...

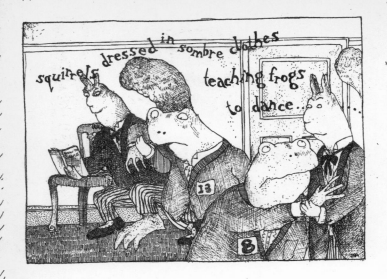

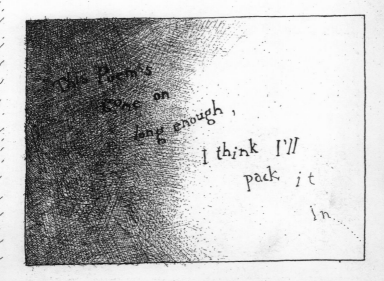

The Unexpected Intelligence of Moles

If you ask a Badger
  If life is exciting,
It goes down its hole
  And answers in writing,
If you ask a Stoat
  If its life is a bore,
It angrily rises
  And shows you the door,

If you ask a Rabbit
    About its affairs,,
It looks at you sideways
    And runs up the stairs,

If you ask an Owl
    Its opinion of wines,
It shuffles its feet
And politely declines,
    But if you ask a Mole
    Any question you like
It will answer succinctly
And always be right.

Happiness

Enjoyment for a rat,
consists of getting fat,

Regularity of habit
is sheer pleasure for
a rabbit,

Dropping things on boats
brings a pang of joy to stoats,

But heaven for a cheetah
is a Lancia three litre.

Budgie

The Budgie
  Lives on fudge. He
  eats so much
    that he can't fly,
    he wonders why.......

FUDGE

The True Life of Rabbits

Rabbits live in luxury,
  In holes beneath the ground,
With air-conditioning, and Hi-Fi
  With quadrophonic sound,

They like to play Monopoly
  And lounge around in suits,

Let the creatures of
the Jungle

Sink their teeth into your uncle,

For when there's nothing left to bite

They'll start on you and that's not right....

If I were you,
I'd leave
Tonight!

Skunk

A Skunk can never know
About its terrible B.O.
It has no helpful friends
to point it out,
The only friends it's got
Are other Skunks,
and they are not
Even aware of what the fuss
is all about.

The Underwater Camel

The Underwater Camel
Lives in lakes and streams and pools,
His hobbies are collecting stamps
    and jumping over stools,
        He likes to wear pyjamas
            And play the slide trombone,
        And if you ring his number
            He'll play it down the 'phone.

Bad Weather

When a Badger goes out in bad weather
He wears a long coat made of leather,
With waterproof socks,
And a large cardboard box
On his head, topped off with a feather.